This toddler talkabout
belongs to

_____

Using this book

Ladybird's toddler talkabouts are ideal for encouraging children to talk about what they see. Bold, colourful pictures and simple questions help to develop early learning skills – such as matching, counting and detailed observation.

Look at this book together. First talk about the pictures yourself, and point out things to look at. Let your child take her* time. With encouragement, she will start to join in, talking about the familiar things in the pictures. Help her to count objects, to look for things that match, and to talk about what is going on in the picture stories.

To avoid the clumsy use of he/she, the child is referred to as 'she'. Toddler talkabouts are suitable for both boys and girls.

Published by Ladybird Books Ltd
80 Strand London WC2R 0RL
A Penguin Company
5 7 9 10 8 6 4

Printed in Italy

I like
cars

illustrated by Richard Morgan
and Terry Burton

Ladybird

Talk about these fast cars.

Do you like to go fast
or slow?

What colours are these cars?

Which is your favourite colour?

This lady needs some petrol. Tell the story.

PETROL

OPEN

1

2

The children are playing – what a noise!

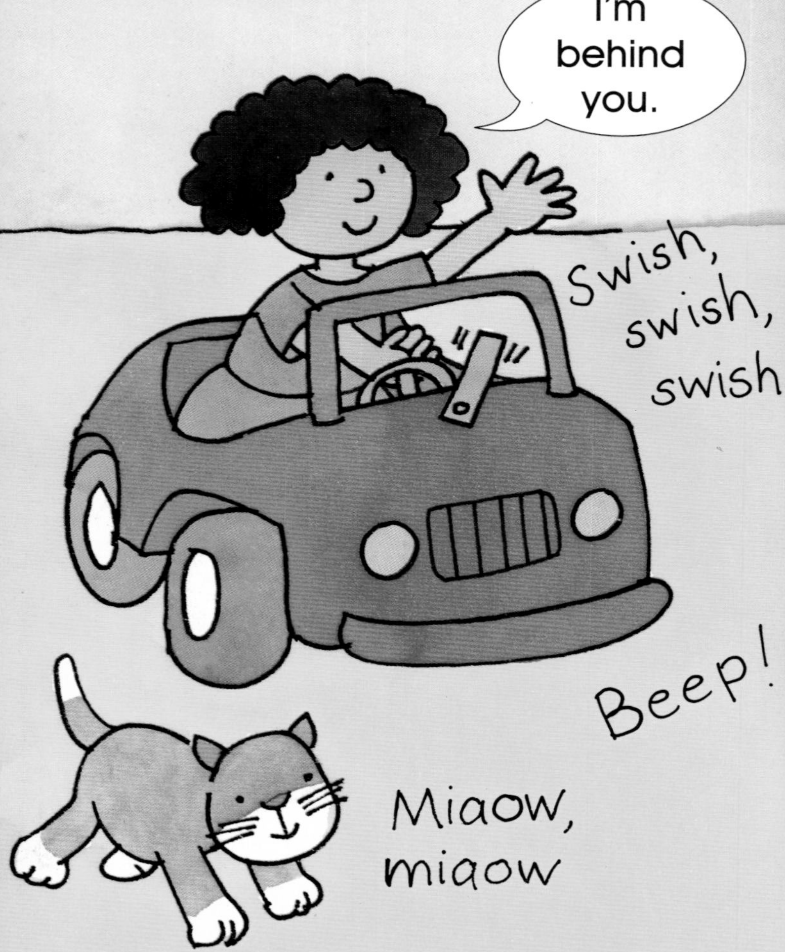

Can *you* make these noises?

Point to the biggest car.

Do you like big cars or little cars?

How many cars are on the transporter?

and downhill...

round the corner...

and through the tunnel!

Look at the pictures and tell the story.

How many red cars...

blue cars...

and yellow cars?

Now count the cars again.

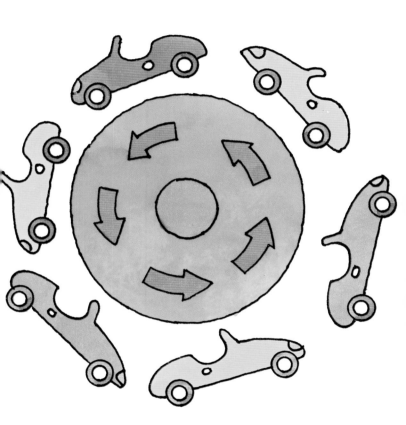

Which car do you like best?

Are there any that you don't like?

What happens when the car breaks down? Tell the story.

1

2